Spotlight on the
MAYA, AZTEC, and INCA CIVILIZATIONS

The Ancient MAYA ECONOMY

Janey Levy

PowerKiDS press™

NEW YORK

Published in 2017 by The Rosen Publishing Group, Inc.
29 East 21st Street, New York, NY 10010

Editor: Caitlin McAneney
Book Design: Mickey Harmon

Photo Credits: Cover Hall, H. Tom/Bridgemanimages.com; p.4 Svetlana Bykova/Shutterstock.com; p. 5 (map) Peter Hermes Furian/Shutterstock.com; p. 6 Hurst Photo/Shutterstock.com; p. 7 soft_light/Shutterstock.com; pp. 8–9 (Maya ruins) Martin M303/Shutterstock.com; p. 9 (left inset) PHAS/Contributor/Universal Images Group/Getty Images; p. 9 (right inset) Insights/Contributor/Getty Images; p. 11 fototehnik/Shutterstock.com; p. 13 DEA PICTURE LIBRARY/De Agostini Picture Library/Getty Images; p. 14 JANET SCHWARTZ/Stringer/AFP/Getty Images; p. 15 klublu/Shutterstock.com; p. 16 De Agostini/W. Buss/De Agostini Picture Library/Getty Images; p. 17 https://en.wikipedia.org/wiki/Chaac#/media/File:MyanRainGodChac0180Rot.jpg; p. 19 Jean du Boisberranger/The Image Bank/Getty Images; p. 20 https://upload.wikimedia.org/wikipedia/commons/8/86/Maya_disks%2C_Mexico%2C_c._550-950_C.E.%2C_jade_inset_with_amazonite%2C_long-term_loan_to_the_Dayton_Art_Institute.jpg;p. 21 https://upload.wikimedia.org/wikipedia/commons/2/21/Maya_jade_plaque.jpg; p. 23 Independent Picture Service/Contributor/Getty Images; p. 24 Diego Lezama/Lonely Planet Images/Getty Images; p. 25 Stefano Ember/Shutterstock.com; p. 26 Martin Froyda/Shutterstock.com; p. 27 Werner Forman/Getty Images; p. 28 Purchase, Joseph Pulitzer Bequest, 1992/The Metropolitan Museum of Art; p. 29 f9photos/Shutterstock.com.

Cataloging-in-Publication Data

Names: Levy, Janey.
Title: The ancient Maya economy / Janey Levy.
Description: New York : PowerKids Press, 2017. | Series: Spotlight on the Maya, Aztec, and Inca civilizations | Includes index.
Identifiers: ISBN 9781499419665 (pbk.) | ISBN 9781499419696 (library bound) | ISBN 9781499419672 (6 pack)
Subjects: LCSH: Mayas--Economic conditions.
Classification: LCC F1435.3.E27 L48 2017 | DDC 320.97281'016--dc23

CPSIA Compliance Information: Batch #BS16PK: For further information contact Rosen Publishing, New York, New York at 1-800-237-9932.

CONTENTS

THE ANCIENT MAYA

The ancient Maya civilization first appeared nearly 4,000 years ago. It emerged around 1800 BC in what's now Central America. By AD 250, the Maya had built a vibrant civilization that stretched from what's today southern Mexico, across modern-day Guatemala and Belize, and into Honduras and El Salvador. This marked the beginning of a brilliant age in ancient Maya civilization called the Classic Period. The civilization flourished until about AD 900, when it began to collapse and the Classic Period came to an end.

The vast Maya territory wasn't a single, unified nation, but a collection of independent **city-states**, each with its own ruler. The great ones such as Tikal and Uxmal rivaled ancient Greek city-states such as Athens. How did the Maya achieve this? Read on to learn how they created their civilization and acquired wealth through an economy based largely on trade.

Tikal

The region occupied by the Maya is often called Mesoamerica. "Meso" means "in the middle," and the name "Mesoamerica" is used because this area lies between North America and South America.

THE WORLD OF THE ANCIENT MAYA

Thick **rain forest** covered the land the Maya occupied, creating a harsh **environment**. Wild animals, including deadly creatures such as rattlesnakes and jaguars, filled the rain forest. During the rainy season, disease-carrying mosquitoes swarmed in huge clouds. In the dry season, water levels fell, and **drought** threatened. In addition, it was difficult to raise crops in the thin topsoil of the rain forest. The necessary **nutrients** were in the plants already growing there, not the soil. It was hard for new crops to get the nutrients they needed to grow properly.

Why would the ancient Maya choose to live here?

Maize was one of the most important crops for the Maya. They used it to make most meals.

Some believe overcrowding in other places forced them into the rain forest. However, the ancient Maya prospered. They settled near rivers, lakes, and swamps. They cleared the forest and grew maize (corn), beans, squash, and other crops. They learned how to use their environment to their advantage to develop a thriving civilization with a strong economy.

The rain forest is a beautiful and fascinating—but often deadly—place.

Over the centuries, the early Maya settlements grew into city-states. About 40 city-states existed during the Classic Period. Some had a population as great as 60,000 or more. Without metal tools or wheeled carts, the Maya mined and moved huge blocks of limestone to build the centers of their city-states. These centers contained temples, pyramids, palaces, plazas, and courts for playing ball. The Maya created stone sculptures and relief, or raised, carvings.

The Maya also developed a hieroglyphic, or picture-based, writing system. They used it to write books called codices on paper they made from the inner bark of wild fig trees.

Ruling each city-state was the *ajaw*, or holy lord, who received his power from the gods. Below him were nobles, and below nobles were commoners. They all served important roles in the economy of their city-state.

The ancient Maya made many carvings of their kings. Today, they still live on in stone.

LORD BIRD JAGUAR IV

KING K'AK' TILIW CHAN YOPAAT

The ancient Maya's great achievements included their **complex** calendar system. It consisted of three calendars: a solar calendar, a sacred calendar, and the Long Count. The solar calendar was 365 days long, just like our modern calendar, because it was based on how long it takes Earth to travel around the sun. It contained 18 months of 20 days each, plus a five-day period considered unlucky.

The 260-day sacred calendar contained 13 **cycles** of 20 named days. The Long Count was a cycle of 5,125 years, with each day individually named. When the cycle ended, the calendar started over.

This calendar system required an equally complex math system. The Maya even developed the concept of zero. This was a great development in mathematics that wouldn't be realized in Europe until much later. Maya mathematical thinking was very advanced, and it contributed to their prosperous economy.

Historians believe the Aztec adopted their calendar from the advanced Maya calendar. This artifact reflects the ancient Aztec calendar.

WHAT'S AN ECONOMY?

As the ancient Maya civilization developed, so did its economy. What's an economy? Simply put, it's the exchange of goods and services. But did you know different types of economies exist?

A barter system is an ancient type of economy in which people exchange goods and services they agree have equal value. In the ancient Maya world, for example, this might mean someone with maize and someone with beans would exchange their goods. In a command type of economy, a central power decides what will be produced, how it will be produced, and who will get it. Finally, there's a market economy. In this system, goods and services are bought and sold using some sort of currency, or money.

Recent research has shown the ancient Maya had both a barter system and a market economy. They had their own forms of currency, although they didn't use money in the way we do today.

Spanish historian and missionary Bartolomé de Las Casas, writing in the 1560s, recorded his observations on the Maya economy.

D. Fr. BARTOLOME DE LAS CASA
Nació en 1474.
Murió en 1566.

AGRICULTURE

Agriculture formed the basis of the Maya economy. At first, the ancient Maya practiced what's called slash-and-burn agriculture. They cleared the forest by burning it. This got rid of weeds and provided ash that acted as fertilizer. They also improved the soil by alternating crops from season to season and allowing fields to lie fallow, or to rest unused for a season. Alternating crops improved soil structure, increased fertility, and helped control weeds,

This is an example of slash-and-burn agriculture. Today, people know that this practice can harm the environment.

In the mountains of Peru, you can still see agricultural terraces created long ago by the Inca, which likely resemble the terraces the Maya carved into the hills of the rain forest.

pests, and diseases. Allowing fields to lie fallow also increased fertility.

As the population grew, the Maya found ways to increase the yield of their crops. They **irrigated**. They **composted**. They built terraces on the hilly rain forest land to create flat surfaces suitable for farming. They filled in swamps to create new fields and fertilized gardens with mud. They formed artificial ponds for raising fish and built pens to hold deer and other game animals they'd captured from the rain forest.

This is one of the walls of the Palace of the Masks at the ancient site of Kabah. It was built for the rain god, Chaac. The highly decorated palace shows the importance of rain to the Maya people.

Anyone who grows crops knows they won't have the same yield every year, even if they plant the same amount of crops. Bad weather, pests, or disease can lead to a poor harvest, while opposite conditions can produce an abundant harvest.

The ancient Maya experienced years of poor harvests and years of abundance. How did they deal with the changing levels in the food supply? Storing the extra food from years of abundance wasn't an option. Stored crops were likely to spoil in the damp rain forest. What could the Maya do to keep people from starving?

Neighboring Maya city-states established networks, or webs, among themselves to move crops where they were needed. If one city-state had an excess, it moved food to a neighbor that didn't have enough to feed its people. The next year, that first city-state might need help from someone else. This early instance of trade helped city-states survive and prosper during difficult times.

Chaac, the rain god, was very important to the Maya because crops needed rain to fall at the right time and in the right quantities.

MAYA TRADE

We know that agriculture played an important part in Maya trade, but many questions remain about the systems the Maya used. What goods were traded, and how were they transported? Were all goods available to all people? Where were goods exchanged? What was used for currency, and who controlled trade?

Experts have suggested trade likely took place on three levels: local, regional, and long distance. Local and regional trade were probably most important for the majority of people. That's because goods from within the area could reach them easily and at a reasonable cost. Such goods included food and other basic supplies.

The size of the area included in local and regional trade depended on geography and politics. For example, the city-state of Tikal controlled a vast area with rivers for easy transport. Therefore, people living in Tikal had access to a great variety of resources.

Just as people today might go to a farmers' market for fresh fruits and vegetables, the ancient Maya got food they couldn't grow themselves at a local market.

These Maya disks were made of jade and tiny pieces of a gem called amazonite.

While local and regional trade supplied basic goods, long-distance trade supplied **exotic** items. Such items included valuable, hard-to-get materials such as obsidian, granite, jade, shells, and feathers. Obsidian is volcanic glass that's commonly black. Granite is another volcanic product that was used by the Maya.

Among the Maya, the word "jade" referred to the mineral jadeite. It came from a single source in eastern Guatemala. Shells, of course, came from coastal regions. The sought-after feathers came from colorful quetzals—birds that occupy mountain forests in the southern Maya region.

You might think only the wealthy owned costly exotic

items. While that was often true, it wasn't always the case. Obsidian blades, which had many practical uses, have been found in the remains of even modest Maya houses. Every household in the small ancient Maya village of Ceren (in modern-day El Salvador) was found to have a jade ax for cutting trees, building, and woodworking.

The Maya made many pieces of jewelry and artwork with green jade.

TRANSPORTING GOODS

How were trade goods transported? You might imagine the ancient Maya used carts or wagons pulled by oxen or horses. But they had no oxen or horses. Christopher Columbus brought the first cattle to the Americas in 1493. The Spanish brought the first horses to Mexico in 1519. Some experts believe this is why the Maya never developed wheeled carts. There was no point, since there were no animals to pull them.

The ancient Maya could either carry goods on their back or use canoes. Canoes were used along the coasts and on rivers because they offered the easiest way to transport goods over long distances. For short distances, or where there weren't **navigable** waterways, people carried the load on their back. A farmer engaged in local trade might carry his own crops. A well-to-do merchant or member of the **elite** might have slaves carry the load.

In the modern Maya world, you may still see women carry large loads to and from the marketplace, often in addition to an infant.

THE ANCIENT MAYA MARKETPLACE

The goods being transported were bound for marketplaces. Originally, marketplaces were simply large open spaces where buyers and sellers gathered to exchange goods. Marketplaces with permanent stone structures didn't appear until the Late Classic Period. Tikal was one of the first sites where archaeologists were able to identify the physical remains of a marketplace. The ruins at Tikal answered many questions about Maya marketplaces and ancient economies in general.

TIKAL RUINS

The ruins of Tikal taught experts a lot about ancient Maya life. It was a huge city-state that was home to more than 60,000 people.

Marketplaces were often located near the center of the city-state. That was the case, for example, at Tikal. However, in some city-states—such as Caracol—marketplaces may have been located around the city's edges.

Records from the 16th century, which was when the Spanish came to the land of the Maya, indicate there were different kinds of merchants in the marketplaces. Some merchants were professional traveling merchants. Others were small-time traders who perhaps didn't travel and who sold small items, such as pins and needles.

What kind of transactions, or exchanges, took place in ancient Maya marketplaces? Barter was common and often used for basic goods. For example, people might trade maize for beans and beans for cacao, which is used to make chocolate. Barter was even used in transactions for exotic goods such as gold, turquoise, and feathers.

Other transactions included currency. This currency wasn't money like we use today. Rather, the Maya used valued items that were easy to carry and could be paid out in an unlimited variety of amounts. Bartolomé de Las Casas, the 16th-century Spanish

Ancient Maya artwork taught historians a lot about which goods were used by both commoners and royalty.

Diego de Landa was responsible for the building of this monastery, San Antonio de Padua, in Mexico. Construction began in 1553 on top of an ancient Maya city.

historian and missionary mentioned earlier, recorded the use of salt as currency. Diego de Landa, another 16th-century Spanish missionary, listed cacao and stone beads as currency. Some Maya in what's today Guatemala used small copper axes, probably imported from Mexico, as currency.

So how did these marketplaces operate? Were there any rules? Did anyone exercise control? Read on to find out.

According to Bartolomé de Las Casas, the elite controlled Maya marketplaces. They scheduled market times, approved the use of space, and charged fines and fees—perhaps even one for access to water.

However, the elite didn't exercise complete control. Marketplaces had managers, although it's not clear if the manager was a member of the elite class or a lower class. Ordinary Maya might have also had control over which marketplaces they preferred.

All levels of ancient Maya society came together in the marketplace, where they enjoyed the benefits of trade. It protected them from food shortages in years of poor harvest. It brought foods they

Maya royalty benefitted from trade as well. They had the finest animal furs and feathers, the most valuable jewelry, and their precious cacao drink.

The Maya left behind both great buildings and small artifacts that give us clues to the way they lived. This is the Pyramid of the Magician in the abandoned city of Uxmal.

couldn't raise themselves and exotic luxury goods to those who could afford them. This **commerce** brought prosperity.

Factors ranging from war to drought led to the collapse of the Classic Period around 900. Most city-states were abandoned. By the time the Spanish arrived in 1519, most Maya were living in small villages.

THE MAYA MARKETPLACE TODAY

Although the great ancient Maya civilization ended, the Maya people didn't disappear. They're still living across their ancient homelands and carrying on many of their ancient traditions—including the marketplace.

If you visit Maya lands today, you'll find two kinds of marketplaces. One provides food and other goods to the local community. Here you'll find maize, which remains an important part of the Maya diet. You'll also find goods such as cloth, which women produce at home to sell at the market.

The second kind is one the ancient Maya might never have imagined—the tourist market. Here you'll find goods the Maya produce to sell to foreign visitors. These goods commonly draw on ancient Maya traditions and art. You'll find purses and table linens made from cloth woven in traditional Maya patterns. You'll find jewelry and wall carvings bearing the likenesses of Maya gods. Here, in these marketplaces, you'll catch a glimpse of the ancient Maya world.

GLOSSARY

city-state (SIH-tee–STAYT): An independent city and the land around it.

commerce (KAH-murs): The large-scale buying and selling of goods and services.

complex (KAHM-plehks): Made up of different parts, sometimes not easy to understand.

compost (KAHM-pohst): To treat land with decayed organic material to make it more fertile.

cycle (SY-kuhl): A repeating period of time.

drought (DROWT): A period of time during which there is very little or no rain.

elite (ih-LEET): The people in a society who are thought to be the greatest.

environment (ehn-VY-ruhn-muhnt): The conditions that surround a living thing and affect the way it lives.

exotic (ihg-ZAH-tihk): From another part of the world.

irrigate (EER-uh-gayt): To supply water to crops.

navigable (NAA-vuh-guh-buhl): Able to be traveled through.

nutrient (NOO-tree-uhnt): Something a living thing needs to grow and stay alive.

rain forest (RAYN FOH-rehst): A tropical forest that gets at least 100 inches (254 cm) of rain a year.

INDEX

PRIMARY SOURCE LIST

Page 9 (left inset): Lintel 16 from Structure 21. Relief carving in limestone. Yaxchilán, State of Chiapas, Mexico. Late Classic Period (AD 600 to 900). Now kept at the British Museum, London, United Kingdom.

Page 16: Detail from the Palace of the Masks. Also known as Codz Poop. Archaeological site of Kabah. Late Classic Period (AD 600 to 900). Located in Yucatán, Mexico.

Page 28: Maya Vessel with Seated Lord. Ceramic and stucco. Created by a Maya artisan in Mexico. Late Classic Period (AD 600 to 900). Now kept at the Metropolitan Museum of Art, New York, New York.

Page 29: Pyramid of the Magician. Built by the Maya people between AD 600 and 1000. Stone. Located at Uxmal, Yucatán, Mexico.

WEBSITES

Due to the changing nature of Internet links, PowerKids Press has developed an online list of websites related to the subject of this book. This site is updated regularly. Please use this link to access the list: www.powerkidslinks.com/soac/mayaec